A Random House book
Published by Random House Australia Pty Ltd
Level 3, 100 Pacific Highway, North Sydney NSW 2060
www.randomhouse.com.au

First published by Random House Australia in 2014

Addresses for companies within the Random House Group can be found at www.randomhouse.com.au/offices

National Library of Australia
Cataloguing-in-Publication Entry

Author: Loughlin, Patrick.
Title: Banana Kick / Patrick Loughlin, with contributions from Billy Slater;
    illustrated by Nahum Ziersch.
ISBN: 978 0 85798 266 7 (pbk)
Series: Billy Slater; 2.
Target Audience: For primary school age.
Subjects: Rugby League football – Juvenile fiction.
        Rugby League football players – Juvenile fiction.
Other Authors/Contributors: Slater, Billy; Ziersch, Nahum, illustrator.
Dewey Number: A823.4

Illustration and design by Nahum Ziersch
Typeset by Midland Typesetters, Australia
Printed in Australia by Griffin Press, an accredited ISO AS/NZS 14001:2004
Environmental Management System printer

Random House Australia uses papers that are natural, renewable and recyclable products and made from wood grown in sustainable forests. The logging and manufacturing processes are expected to conform to the environmental regulations of the country of origin.

# BANANA KICK

WRITTEN BY
**PATRICK LOUGHLIN**

ILLUSTRATED BY
**NAHUM ZIERSCH**

RANDOM HOUSE AUSTRALIA

# BILLY SLATER

I was pretty small when I first started playing footy and didn't have the natural strength or size the other players had. But I knew I loved the game, so I had to find other skills to help me succeed. Even now, I still work on things like my speed and my ball handling. I also try to eat healthy and stay fit in order to perform at the highest level.

It may take some players a while to work out where their talents lie, so it's really important to encourage your team-mates and to respect your opponents. After all, footy is not very exciting without an opposition! It can also be fun to give people nicknames, but you have to make sure those names don't hurt their feelings. You're always going to play your best if you feel confident and relaxed on the field.

In *Banana Kick* you will read about how Junior finds a way to help his team succeed, but soon becomes discouraged by other people's comments. He's bigger than most players, prompting some to think his size is an unfair advantage. Junior needs a little encouragement from his friends and family to feel comfortable in his own skin and to have fun playing football again.

I hope you enjoy reading *Banana Kick* and understand that there is often more to people than meets the eye. Everyone is different, and that's one of the best things about playing in a team.

**Billy Slater**

# A TIGHT FIT

It was another beautiful Saturday. The sky was a bright blue and the crowd of spectators at the West Hill Ravens home ground was enjoying the early morning sunshine, which was taking the bite out of the frosty May air.

The only ones not enjoying the morning were the West Hill Ravens Under 11s. They were huddled glumly behind their goalposts as the goal kicker for the Burnsfield Bears attempted to convert the Bears' second try in ten minutes.

< 1 >

'This is pathetic!' whined Corey. 'You guys need to learn how to tackle. We're getting creamed!'

'I didn't see *you* stop anyone from scoring!' said the Ravens fullback. His name was Cameron Cotter, but everyone called him C. C. for short.

'Hey, they didn't score on *my* side. I had my guy well-covered.'

'We're not going to win this game by arguing with each other,' said their captain, Liam McGill. 'These guys keep pushing us back. We just need to get out of our half.'

There were a few mumbles of agreement from the team, and some loud grumbling from Corey. But Junior Taafuli stood quietly

< 2 >

at the back of the huddle, watching his team-mates and saying nothing.

At ten years of age, Junior was already five foot five. His hefty Samoan build had earned him the nickname Mount Taafuli. While he looked intimidating to the opposition, Junior was actually a quiet kid. He always had been. But that didn't mean he had nothing on his mind.

As Junior watched the ball sail over the posts, bringing the score to 18–0, he was busy thinking, *I really wish this jersey wasn't so tight.*

When Coach Steve had handed out the jerseys at the start of the season, Junior had been given the number eight jersey. Last year's Under 11s prop forward must have

< **3** >

been much smaller, because Junior struggled to even get the jersey on. Rather than
tell Coach Steve, though, Junior just nodded
and smiled. He didn't want to make a fuss.

For the first four games of the season,
Junior wore a jersey far too small for him.
He didn't complain once, even when it
meant he could barely raise his arms to take
a pass. It didn't make running easy, either.

It was only because Junior was sitting
right in front of him at half-time that Coach
Steve noticed his awkward slouching.
Coach would usually be revving the boys up,
but after one win and one draw from four
starts *and* 18–0 at half-time, even Coach was
at a loss as to how to get the season back on
track. Having a bye the week before hadn't

< 4 >

helped, either. While deep in thought, he glanced down at Junior, who looked like the life was being squeezed out of him.

'Junior, have you grown?' asked Coach. 'That jersey looks two sizes too small.'

Junior tried to shrug, then looked even more uncomfortable. A couple of the other boys glanced over and sniggered.

Coach Steve turned to the Ravens prop forward. 'Poppa, swap jerseys with Junior.'

'But I'm number ten!' protested Poppa.

'That's okay,' Junior mumbled. 'It doesn't matter.'

'Nonsense, you can hardly breathe in that thing,' said Coach Steve. 'Swap jerseys, you two. Quick sticks!'

The boys reluctantly swapped jerseys.

< 5 >

'This has a rip in the armpit,' groaned Poppa, dangling Junior's jersey out in front of him like a rotten fish.

'Sorry, bro,' Junior said in a soft voice that didn't quite match his size. But secretly he was glad. Poppa's jersey was much more comfortable.

No one, least of all Junior Taafuli, realised the difference that a change of jerseys would make to the outcome of the match — and the rest of the Ravens' season.

Suddenly, Junior could breathe.

< 6 >

# THE MAGIC OFF-LOAD

When the Ravens received the ball from the kick-off, Junior was the first forward to take a hit-up. He ran five metres before two Bears players moved in from either side. It was a team-tackle sandwich but Junior didn't go down. He just took the two players with him.

When a third Bears player tackled low to stop Junior's legs, Junior still kept going. One step at time, he dragged the player along the ground like an annoying piece of toilet paper.

< 7 >

Then a fourth Bears player came in over the top. This time, Junior did go down. But the damage was done. The Ravens had made a twenty-metre gain!

Junior's success inspired the rest of the team. Suddenly, the forwards were pushing forward and out-muscling the defence. The Miller twins, who didn't have Junior's size but were still tall and lanky for their age, took the next two runs and made another twenty metres between them.

The tryline was in sight.

On the last tackle, Liam put a rolling grubber through to the in-goal. Corey outraced everyone to the ball, diving on it to score just before the ball rolled dead.

The Ravens supporters erupted. The Bears stood in silence. Coach Steve was

< 8 >

running back and forth, flapping his arms and screaming, 'Ravens, fly!'

There was a smile on the face of every Ravens player.

'Great run, Junior,' said Liam, jogging over to high-five the team.

'Must be *my* jersey,' added Poppa.

Azza threw an arm around Junior. 'You reckon you can do that again?'

Junior smiled. 'I think so.'

But the next time Junior got the ball, he didn't stop at twenty metres. He just kept on going.

And going.

And going.

Every time another tackler came in, he'd stop for a moment and then slowly

< 9 >

start moving forward again. He lumbered over the opposition like a four-stroke lawn-mower. It took six players to finally pull him down, and by the time they did Junior had made thirty metres.

Before the Ravens knew it, they were back in the opposition's twenty, and it wasn't long before the Ravens were crossing the line again. A quick-thinking dummy from Liam allowed him to sneak through the defence and score straight under the posts. Liam lined up the kick and easily sailed the ball over the black dot. The score was now locked at 18–18.

'Wow.' Jackson smiled. 'We're totally back –'

'In this, thanks to Junior,' said Matthew,

< 10 >

finishing his twin brother's sentence. 'That was awesome, dude!'

'Yeah, you totally tore through them like a bowling ball!' said Jackson, and everyone cracked up. 'What's so funny?'

'Bowling ball?' said Tai. 'More like a *cannonball*. A human cannonball!'

The others laughed. Junior smiled and got back into position. He wasn't finished just yet.

On the next set of six, Azza moved into dummy half and called for a runner.

'Give it to Cannonball!' yelled Tai.

Azza fired a long, flat pass to Junior, who came steaming in through the middle of the forward pack like a Spanish bull let loose on a crowd of tourists.

< 11 >

The Bears' faces dropped. Junior burst through them at speed. They jumped on his back, they grabbed at his legs, they yanked at his shorts and tugged at his jersey, but Junior didn't stop. Even with all the Bears focused on stopping Junior, Junior managed to lob a one-handed pass back to Blake 'the Fake' Vargas.

Blake sped off with the ball. With most of the opposition still clinging to Junior, there was only the fullback left to beat. Blake drew the fullback with a sly sidestep and then slipped the ball to C. C., who ran thirty metres to score another try for the Ravens.

Coach Steve stood on the sidelines grinning from ear to ear. When the final whistle blew, the score was 22–18.

< 12 >

'What a win, boys!' said Coach. 'That was probably one of the best comebacks by a Ravens team I've ever seen. And I've seen a few.'

'How about that off-load by Cannonball to C. C.?' said Tai.

'That off-load was magic, Junior. Sheer magic,' said Coach Steve. 'I'm going to start calling you Merlin, if you keep that up.'

'Who?' asked the boys.

'Merlin. You kids haven't heard of Merlin the wizard?'

'I've heard of Harry Potter,' said Azza. 'He's magic.'

'Fine. I'll start calling you Harry Potter, then. Anyway, I have a very good feeling about the rest of our season if we play like

< **14** >

that every week,' said Coach Steve, and he winked at Junior.

Junior smiled.

The Ravens walked off the ground to applause from their parents and supporters, and headed towards the change sheds. But just before Junior stepped inside he over-heard a Bears supporter say, 'What's a kid that size doing in the Under 11s anyway? There should be a rule against kids that big playing. One of our boys could get seriously hurt!'

Junior didn't have to stop and ask. He knew straight away they were talking about him. Junior's smile vanished. His eyes fell to the ground and the magic off-load was as good as forgotten.

< 15 >

# 3
# BILLY'S CHALLENGE

It was a cool May afternoon, and even though the Under 11s had only just begun training, the sun was already sinking behind the hills. Junior and the rest of the team were running warm-up laps around the Ravens field.

'All right, one more lap will do it,' called Coach Steve.

'Are you kidding, Coach? We've already done *four*,' panted Jackson.

'That's right, and one more will make five. Now, less whining and more running!'

< 16 >

Sometimes Coach Steve seemed to enjoy torturing the boys at training, but Junior didn't mind. He thought Coach was funny, and he could handle running laps even if he was usually at the back of the pack. *After all, what's the rush?* thought Junior. *A lap is a lap, no matter how fast you run.*

When Junior finished his final lap, he jogged over to join the rest of the team on the side of the field. He was a little surprised to see Billy Slater standing there spinning a football in one hand.

'We're very fortunate to have our mentor, the one and only Billy Slater, here today to share his amazing knowledge of the game with us,' said Coach Steve, and the boys all cheered.

< **17** >

'Billy, are we going to practise taking bombs?' asked Poppa.

'I thought we were going to run new set plays,' said Liam.

'But I want to see Billy's sidestep again,' said Blake.

Billy chuckled. 'Relax, fellas. There'll be plenty of time for all that in a minute. First, I want to talk to you about nutrition.'

'New what?' asked Jack Monroe, the Ravens lock, who prided himself on never having finished a book in his six years of school life.

'Nutrition — as in nutrients, commonly found in fresh food,' said Ravi, the Ravens' only reserve. He prided himself on reading

< 18 >

lots of books at school and at home and even on weekends.

'Why would you want to eat tree ants?' asked Jack, a puzzled look on his face.

'OMG! It's NU-TRI-ENTS, not NEW TREE ANTS!' exclaimed Ravi. 'Stuff like protein and calcium and vitamins and minerals.'

'Well, why didn't you just say that?' said Jack.

Billy decided it was time to step in. 'Anyway, since I've been attending your training sessions, I've noticed some of the snacks you guys eat. Coach Steve and I are a little concerned about all the junk food you consume.'

Junior looked down at the grass. *Here it comes*, he thought. Junior had always been bigger than the other kids, and every time food came up at school, everyone seemed to look at him.

Except no one did this time. They were too busy watching Billy.

'You probably know that a bad diet can make you unhealthy, right?'

< 20 >

'Yeah,' agreed some of the boys.

'But did you know that eating junk food can affect how you play footy?' asked Billy.

'Like if you get too fat, like Coach Steve, you won't be able to run laps,' said Tai.

'Watch it, Tai!' grumbled Coach Steve.

'Um, no. Not really,' said Billy, trying not to laugh. 'It's all about fuel. Just like cars, our bodies need the right kind of fuel to function at their best. And guess what, boys? Junk food is *not* the best fuel. Who can tell me why?'

Ravi's hand shot up in the air. 'Too much sugar and fat and not enough nutrients.'

'Where does he get this stuff?' Jack asked no one in particular.

< 21 >

'Ravi's spot on,' said Billy. 'It's about balance. That's why we're going to have a little challenge to see if you boys can give junk food the flick for one week.'

Coach Steve began to hand out yellow cards. 'Everyone gets ONE, so don't lose them!' he instructed.

Junior looked down at the little yellow card in his hands.

## HEALTHY SNACK CHALLENGE

| | Mon | Tues | Wed | Thur | Fri | Sat | Sun |
|---|---|---|---|---|---|---|---|
| **HEALTHY SNACKS.** [e.g. fruit, vegetables and yoghurt] | | | | | | | |
| **JUNK FOOD.** [e.g. chips, chocolate and lollies] | | | | | | | |

< 22 >

'This looks like homework!' Jack gasped in horror.

'I guess it is, in a way,' said Billy.

'Homework for footy? That's got to be illegal!' Tai splapped his head in disgust.

Billy laughed. 'You're probably right, Tai. Don't worry, I'm not going to mark you on spelling or anything. The challenge is to eat the right foods – something from all five food groups.'

'That's easy,' interrupted Tai. 'I eat the five food groups every day – pizza, nuggets, chips, chocolate and ice-cream!'

Everyone laughed.

Billy smiled. 'Hmm. Not sure where you've been getting your info, Tai, but they are *not* the five food groups.'

< **23** >

'Are you sure?' asked Tai, grinning widely.

'Pretty sure. Look, all you need to do is try to replace any unhealthy snacks like chips, chocolate and biscuits, with healthy ones like fruit, nuts or vegetables.'

'So, in other words, we have to eat boring, tasteless food?' asked Corey.

'It may taste good, Corey, but if food comes wrapped in plastic, it's probably not very good for you,' said Billy.

'That's all right,' said Tai. 'Pizza comes in a cardboard box!'

Coach Steve sighed. 'What is it with you kids and pizza?'

The boys laughed again, but Junior just stared blankly at the empty boxes on the

< 24 >

card waiting to be filled in. He had a bad feeling about those boxes.

< 25 >

# 4
# LITTLE CARD, BIG TROUBLE

'Junior! Dinnertime!' called Ramona, Junior's older sister.

There was no answer.

At that exact moment Junior was lying on his bed and watching one of his favourite rappers on YouTube.

'JUNIOR!'

This time Junior did hear Ramona, along with most of the neighbourhood. 'Coming!' he called back.

He closed the laptop and was about to

< 26 >

leave when he noticed the little yellow card lying on the floor. The bold black words on the card jumped out at him.

## HEALTHY SNACK CHALLENGE

Junior sighed and shoved it in his pocket, then headed into the living room.

Because Junior's mum worked at the hospital and his dad worked long hours at the fruit market, it was often Ramona who did the cooking during the week. Sometimes Junior and his other sister, Mele, helped her.

'There you are, Junior. Where have you been?' said Ramona. 'Can you call the boys? They're outside.'

< 27 >

Junior walked to the back door and yelled to his younger brothers, Joseph and Feleti. 'Hey, boys! Dinner!'

'Junior!' cried Joseph, the youngest in the family. 'Come play with us!'

'Yeah! Tackle us!' pleaded Feleti.

Junior laughed. 'All right. One tackle, then dinner.' He could rarely refuse his younger brothers.

A moment later six-year-old Joseph was steaming towards him with the football. Unlike Junior, both of his brothers were little and skinny. Junior easily cut Joseph off, grabbing hold of him by the waist and turning him upside down. Joseph still managed to throw a pass to Feleti, but Junior was too quick and soon had Feleti

< 28 >

wrapped up in his other arm. The three of them toppled to the ground, giggling.

'All right, you're tackled. Now, go wash your hands for dinner,' said Junior, pushing his brothers off him.

'Tickle monster,' insisted Joseph, jumping onto Junior's back.

'No tickle monster, dinner!' replied Junior.

'Hey, what's this?' said Feleti.

Junior wrestled Joseph away and looked around to find Feleti standing in front of him waving his yellow card. 'Hey, that's mine,' said Junior. 'Give it here.'

'You'll have to chase me!' Feleti laughed and took off for the house. This time he was too fast for Junior.

< 29 >

Joseph squealed, following as Junior gave chase. By the time Junior got to the back step, Feleti was inside and tearing down the hall, waving the card as he went. When Junior reached the kitchen, he found Ramona holding the card instead of Feleti.

'What's this?' asked Ramona.

'Nothin'. Just some homework,' said Junior, breathing hard. He glared at Feleti, who was smirking from behind the safety of his big sister.

'From school?' quizzed Ramona.

'Yep,' said Junior.

'So, why does it have the West Hill Ravens emblem on the other side?' Ramona pointed at the familiar symbol of a black bird with its wings outstretched.

< 30 >

'Um.' Junior wasn't exactly sure why he'd lied about what the card was for. It had just seemed easier, the way not mentioning the healthy snack challenge seemed easier. Junior had managed to *not* mention it to his family for three days.

'Junior, what's it really for?' asked Ramona.

'It's just a thing we have to do for footy,' Junior said reluctantly.

Ramona looked unconvinced. 'Why did you lie about it, then?'

'Lie about what?' asked his mother, appearing behind them.

*Oh great,* thought Junior. *Here's trouble.*

< 31 >

# 5
# MAMA ALWAYS KNOWS BEST

Mama Taafuli, like all mothers, knew how to walk into a room at exactly the worst possible moment. With just one hot look, her eyes told Ramona:

**WHATEVER YOU HAVE, GIVE IT TO ME NOW!**

Ramona immediately handed her mother the yellow card.

Junior's mum was a big lady with big

< 32 >

opinions. She worked long hours as a mater-
nity nurse and she was never shy about
sharing her opinions with new mothers. She
looked at the card and clucked her tongue
dramatically. Then her eyes locked on to
Junior like an infra-red laser sight. 'What is
this all about, Junior?'

For just a moment, Junior thought he
could see steam rising from her head. As
it turned out, it was just the steam from
the rice cooker sitting behind his mother.
'Um . . .'

'I'm waiting, child.'

'Footy,' Junior finally blurted. 'It's for
Billy Slater.'

< 34 >

'So, now your coach and Mr Foot-a-ball star Billy Slater are trying to tell me how to feed you,' said Mama Taafuli, sitting down to the dinner table. 'I know what to feed my children!'

Junior's dad nodded slowly in agreement. He was a tall, strong man, and a gentle father. In fact, he was very much like Junior – a man of few words. He usually let his wife do the talking.

'I don't think it's like that, Mum. It's just a way of encouraging the team to eat healthy snacks,' said Ramona. 'It's not a big deal.'

'Why was it hidden from us, then?' asked their mother. 'What's really going on here, Junior? And no more lying.'

< **35** >

Junior looked at his mother, then down at the table and sighed. 'I just didn't want anyone to see what I eat.'

'Why? Are you sneaking junk food home?' asked his mother, squinting at Junior like a television detective interrogating a suspect.

'No, Mum. It's just . . . what some of the other kids on the team have been saying. And people at last week's game.'

This time his father did speak. 'What did they say, son?'

'You know – that I'm too big for my age.' Junior frowned at the table.

Mama Taafuli's face softened, and she smiled. 'Junior, you silly boy. Did your teammates or those other people give birth to you? No. Who do you think gave birth to

< 36 >

you? Me! I gave birth to you. And you were a big baby. A *very* big baby.'

Junior's brothers giggled at this, and Junior shrank further into his chair.

'Now you are a big boy. Surprise! You're Samoan. You're supposed to be big!' said Mama Taafuli.

Junior kept his eyes down and wondered how long this was going to take. *I hope she doesn't start wagging her finger,* he thought. *Anything but the finger.*

Of course, when he glanced up, his mother's finger was right there, wagging furiously in his face. 'Don't listen to what those people say! Listen to me and to your family,' she said. 'Be proud of who you are, Junior. You're a beautiful boy.'

< 37 >

Junior blushed and rolled his eyes. 'Oh, Mum.'

'Ha! Junior's pretty,' laughed Joseph.

'And don't worry about this little card. You show them how healthy you are,' said Mama Taafuli, slapping one hand on the table and making her knife and fork bounce up into the air and crash back down with a *clank*. 'Now, who wants dessert? *Fa'alifu fai!* Green bananas. Very healthy!' she declared, getting up from the table.

'Yay!' cried Joseph and Feleti.

Junior let out a deep breath. When it comes to their children, Samoan mothers always know best, and you should never try to tell them otherwise.

< 38 >

# 6
# CANNONBALL RUNNING

**'OooOOOoHHHHH!'**

The entire crowd gasped as the mountainous kid in the snugly fit number ten Ravens jersey smashed through another tackle.

It was Round 7 and the Ravens Under 11s were up against the Mount Macquarie Lions, who had also struggled to win a game this season. It didn't look like today was going to be their day, either.

'Run, Junior! Run!' called Azza and

< **39** >

Liam and Tai as Junior made another tackle-busting burst through the opposition defence. But Junior didn't run, he steam-rolled like a bulldozer.

By half-time the Ravens were up 10–4, and there were some low mumblings in the crowd, mostly from the Lions supporters.

'Look at the size of him!' said one surly father.

'He shouldn't be playing in this age group – he's twice their size,' tutted a woman wearing a T-shirt that read 'Go Tyson! Lions are #1'.

'There ought to be a weight division. He probably weighs as much as me,' said a man with long sideburns.

< 40 >

As the Ravens gathered in the middle of the field to listen to Coach Steve, it was hard not to feel the heavy glares of the Lions supporters. Most of their glares were aimed at one Raven in particular.

Junior glanced around at the sea of angry faces.

'I don't think the Lions fans are very happy,' Josh said nervously.

'Don't worry, they'll get over it,' said Coach Steve. 'We just need to focus on the game. It's not over yet. It's a game of halves, remember.'

'What does that even mean?' grumbled Corey.

'It means there are two halves in a game of footy,' said Liam.

< **41** >

'Yeah, you're the halfback, Liam, and I'm five-eighth — two halves. Get it?' Tai laughed, impressed with himself.

Corey groaned. 'Hee-lair-re-us.'

'Do you get it? We're the halves,' said Tai, pointing at himself and Liam and bouncing his eyebrows up and down.

'I get it,' said Corey. 'It's just not funny.'

'It's a bit funny,' said Liam, and Tai nodded crazily in agreement.

'Boys, focus,' said Coach Steve. 'Now, how are we going to stay on top in the second half?'

'Easy-peasy, Coach. We just give it to Cannonball,' said Tai. He motioned to Junior, who was quietly slurping on an orange at the back of the huddle.

< 42 >

Coach turned to him. 'Think you have a few more hit-ups in you, Junior?'

'Yes, Coach,' Junior said quietly.

'Great, 'cause you are having a blinder!' Coach Steve said with a wink. 'Boys, you know what time it is . . .' Coach began flapping his arms wildly. 'Let's flyyyy!' he hollered, and the whole team cheered.

In the second half Junior continued his tackle-busting breaks with the same devastating results. Inspired by their not-so-secret weapon, all the Ravens rose to the challenge. They were tackling harder, running faster and throwing passes like there was no tomorrow, scoring try after try.

< **43** >

The points piled up, and before anyone knew it, the score was 20–10. It was turning into a thumping, and the Lions supporters were not happy. But it was when Junior managed to run through every single Lions player and carry three over the line with him as he scored under the posts that the crowd turned ugly.

For Junior, it was as easy as running through his little brothers in the backyard.

< 44 >

For the Ravens supporters, it was one of the most memorable solo tries they'd ever seen. For the Mount Macquarie Lions fans, it was the final insult.

'Cannonball, Cannonball, Cannonball!' chanted the Ravens.

'BOOOOOOOOOOO!' Every one of the Lions fans seemed to join in. Then the insults started flying – all in the direction of Junior Taafuli.

Junior put his head down and tried to ignore it.

When the final whistle blew, Coach Steve decided to get his team off the ground as quickly as possible. But to Junior, the twenty metres to the change sheds felt like forever. It was as if he were walking in slow motion.

< 45 >

The insults blurred into a continuous dull roar and so did the faces of the Lions supporters. They all seemed to be thinking the same thing.

*Am I a freak?* Junior wondered as he stepped into the safety of the visitors' change sheds. The Ravens may have won the match, but Junior didn't feel like much of a winner.

< 47 >

# 7
# THE STING

'Get those legs up and keep 'em up! I'm talking six inches off the ground!' yelled Coach Steve. 'They don't call this one the gut-buster for nothing!'

There was a chorus of groans from the patch of oval where the Under 11s were running through some strength and conditioning exercises. It was the team's least favourite part of training.

'Just twenty more seconds . . . nineteen, eighteen, eighteen, eighteen . . .'

< 48 >

'C'mon, Coach, you're killing us!' wheezed Jackson.

'Sorry, what was that, Jackson? Oh, now I've lost count. Where was I? Oh yes, nineteen, eighteen, eighteen . . .'

More groans of agony.

'Good one, Jackson!' muttered Corey.

'All right, boys, on your feet,' said Coach Steve. But just as the boys were breathing a sigh of relief, he added, 'We'll finish with ten burpees.'

'Coach, I can't take any more!' pleaded Josh.

'Oh, all right. Just five, then.' Coach smiled. 'Five *sets* of ten.'

'ARRRRGGHHHHHH!'

Coach was rarely satisfied until he heard

< 49 >

at least one tormented scream per training session.

Junior never screamed, and he never complained or pleaded with Coach to stop. It wasn't that he liked the exercises. They were torture. *Worse* than torture. But Junior had been raised to be respectful to his elders. You didn't ask, you just did. At the end of the day he trusted that Coach made them do what was needed to make them a better team.

'All right, let's see if all these healthy snacks you guys are meant to be eating are helping with your tackling,' said Coach. 'Don't forget I'll be collecting those cards today to see if any of you have managed a week without junk food.'

The boys lined up and, one by one, hit up

< 50 >

the large canvas tackling bag that Coach was holding.

'I can't wait to see what Junior's been eating, given his form lately,' Coach said with a chuckle.

'Yeah, he's on a seafood diet: *see* food and eat it,' Corey said under his breath so that Coach couldn't hear.

But Junior heard him. He turned around to say something back, but no words came out.

It was always like this. Junior could run through a pack of menacing forwards. He could even get through Coach Steve's gut-busting exercises. But when it came to words, those casually cruel things that others say, sometimes that sting could last longer and bite deeper than a thousand burpees.

< 51 >

# THE QUIET TYPE

'Back off, Corey,' said Liam. 'Junior's the reason we've won the last two games.'

'Yeah, we wouldn't have played half as good without Cannonball,' added Tai.

'Cannonball?' Corey made a face. 'Looks more like a beachball to me.'

Junior stared back at Corey but remained silent. He could feel the anger bubbling deep down inside him. But he wasn't like his mum. He didn't know how to get the words out.

'Don't let him talk to you like that,

< 52 >

Junior,' said Liam when Corey took his turn at the tackling bag. 'You need to stand up to him, or he'll be at it the whole season.'

Junior shrugged. 'He doesn't scare me, he just has a big mouth.'

'Yeah, he can be a bit painful but he's not all bad,' said Liam. 'Besides, he's a great centre. I think that's why he's been giving you such a hard time lately.'

'What do you mean?' asked Junior, puzzled.

'You know, because you're playing so well and stealing the attention.'

'But I don't even want the attention!'

'I know, you're the quiet type.' Liam laughed. 'That's okay. I hate talking in front of my class at school. But sometimes you

< 53 >

have to defend yourself, or guys like Corey will keep pushing you around. You don't want to be a pushover, do you?'

Junior shook his head. Liam nodded, then ran off for his turn at the tackling bag. Corey trotted back and shot Junior a glance, but Junior just looked away.

*Is Corey really jealous of me?* he wondered. It didn't make much sense. Corey was an amazing player and super-fast. Why would he be jealous of Junior? Liam's words echoed in his head. *Because you're stealing all the attention.*

'Okay, team, we've got a big game this Saturday,' said Coach. 'Let's see if we can

< 54 >

keep this roll we're on going. Last week was great, but everyone's going to have to play at their best to beat the Hawks. They're not coming second by luck.'

'That's okay, Coach, we've got Junior. The Hawks don't stand a chance,' said Tai.

'I'm so sick of you going on about Junior all the time!' said Corey. 'There are other players on this team, you know.'

Tai held up his hands. 'I'm just saying he's been playing well lately.'

'What's the point of winning if we get booed when we walk off the ground?' added Corey, throwing a squinty-eyed glare Junior's way.

'That's enough. No one likes getting booed, least of all Junior,' said Coach Steve.

< 55 >

'Yeah, who cares what a bunch of sore losers think, anyway,' exclaimed Azza. 'It's not like our fans are booing us.'

'They might if *someone* makes us the most hated team in the comp!' said Corey.

'Corey, just forget about it,' said Coach Steve, trying not to lose his patience. He looked over at Junior. 'If you want to be a good footy player, you can't let these things get to you.'

He was speaking to Corey, but looking directly at Junior. The only problem was, Junior wasn't looking back. Instead, he was staring at the shadows cast by the floodlights and worrying about what would happen if he played well again on Saturday.

< 56 >

# 9
# BLOWING OFF STEAM

'Junior, are you in there?' Mele called through the bathroom door.

Junior paused for a moment. 'Um, sort of,' he said finally.

'What do ya mean "sort of"? What are you doing? What's with all this steam?' asked Mele.

*She is so nosy!* 'I'm just having a shower,' Junior called back.

Junior *did* have the shower running, along with the tap in the sink. Both hot water taps

< 57 >

were turned all the way, which was why the room was full of steam. He wasn't in the shower, though. He was dressed in his mother's thick and very pink bathrobe.

He'd seen an ad on TV where a large man got into a sauna and came out as a young child. Junior knew it was meant to be funny, but he thought it was worth a try. If he could shrink himself a little before Saturday, maybe people would stop commenting on his size.

As Junior stood there sweating in his homemade sauna, he was beginning to wonder if it was worth it.

'Why are you having a shower at three-thirty in the afternoon?' asked Mele. 'That's weird.'

< 58 >

'What's weird?' Junior heard Ramona ask.

*Great, this is all I need,* thought Junior. *She must have just arrived home from uni.*

'Junior's having a shower and making a lot of steam!' said Mele.

'At three-thirty?' said Ramona.

Junior rolled his eyes.

'That's what I said,' said Mele.

'How long has he been in there?'

'Ages.'

'Junior, finish your shower and open this door. Mum's gonna kill you if you waste all the hot water,' said Ramona.

Junior quickly turned off the taps and was about to open the door when he remembered what he was wearing. *Good one, Junior.*

< 59 >

*How are you going to explain this?* 'Um, I can't come out. I forgot to bring my clothes in.'

'Just get out here or we're coming in!' yelled Ramona.

His eldest sister wasn't just nosy like Mele, she was pushy as well. Sometimes it felt like Junior had three mothers instead of one. Junior decided to give up and slowly opened the bathroom door.

A waft of steam burst from the bathroom. His sisters took one look at him and fell to the floor with laughter.

'What were you thinking, Junior?' asked Ramona, after she and Mele had finally

< **61** >

recovered from a fit of hysterics. The three of them were sitting on Ramona's bed.

Junior explained how he'd got the idea to give himself a steam bath.

'Junior, that ad's a joke,' said Mele. 'You're not a pair of jeans or a T-shirt – you can't shrink yourself overnight with a bit of steam!'

'I guess not,' said Junior. 'Are you guys going to tell Mum?'

Both girls looked at each other. 'No,' said Ramona. 'But, Junior, don't try to be something you're not, and don't ever change yourself for anyone. You are a big, beautiful Samoan boy who's good at footy and rapping.'

Junior's eyes widened with surprise.

< 62 >

'Yeah, I can hear you every night through the wall, genius,' said Ramona. 'Anyway, if people can't accept you for who you are, then who needs them? You've got us.'

'And we can always whip your butt in footy any day,' Mele said with a laugh.

Junior got up off his sister's bed. 'Okay, no more steaming,' he said, and turned to leave the room.

'Junior?'

'Yeah?'

'I think you should probably take Mum's robe off before she gets home, hey?'

< 63 >

# 10
# ALL ABOARD THE JUNIOR TRAIN

'I can see what they mean – he is HUGE!'

'What do they call him? Cannonball? I think he's backfired today.'

Junior tried to ignore the two Hawks players sledging him right to his face as both teams took to the field for the second half.

The Harbourside Hawks had beaten the Ravens 12–6 in the first round, and this game looked like it would go the same way. The Ravens were down 12–0 and they hadn't even come close to scoring.

< 64 >

The truth was, Junior didn't have the same level of energy he'd had in the last two games. Every time he took up the ball, he'd think about the booing and insults from the week before and he'd slow down to a trot. Then a few Hawks players would drag him to the ground without a fight.

'Don't let them get to you, Junior,' said Liam, watching the two Hawks players high five each other and run into position.

And Junior tried not to — until thirteen minutes into the second half, when the Hawks had skipped to a 16–0 lead. That was when the Hawks halfback said something that made Junior see ten shades of red.

Junior was lining up to take a run and the halfback, a cocky blond kid with a face

< 65 >

full of freckles, was standing at first marker having just made a tackle on the Ravens lock, Jack Monroe. The halfback had outplayed and out-tackled the Ravens all day and he'd also out-sledged everyone on the field.

'Hey, number ten!' called the halfback. 'Is everyone in your family as fat as you? 'Cause I heard the coconut doesn't fall far from the tree!'

Calling Junior fat was one thing, but saying something about his family . . . Something inside Junior snapped. One second he was catching a short pass from Azza at dummy half, and the next second he was running over that little blond halfback. But Junior didn't stop there. He ran through the next player. And the one after that.

< 66 >

He was a steam train collecting passengers one by one. By the time he got near the tryline, Junior had six players riding on his back trying to bring him to a halt. The rest of the Hawks were scattered behind him.

When he arrived at the tryline, Junior swung around 180 degrees, bodies hanging from him like flags on a flagpole. He tossed the ball to a smiling Tai, who gladly dived over to score.

'Way to go, Cannonball!' Tai cheered, jumping aboard Junior's back himself.

But Junior, who should have felt on top of the world, felt as small as a stone in the sea. As he looked around the ground, he didn't notice the cheering faces of the Ravens supporters. All he saw were the cold stares

< **67** >

of the Hawks fans. They weren't booing, but Junior could see the anger written all over their faces.

'All right, guys, this is it! Another quick try and we're back in the game,' shouted Liam, trying to rev up the team.

But while the next try did happen quickly, it was the Hawks – not the Ravens – who scored.

Junior had been staring at the crowd when the Hawks kicked the ball back. He didn't even notice the ball come sailing towards him until it was too late. He threw his arms out to take it, but the ball bounced off the tips of his fingers and struck the ground in front of him. He'd knocked on right in front of the tryline.

< 68 >

The Hawks packed the scrum quickly, and before anyone knew it, their halfback snuck through a gap in the Ravens' backline to score. Junior watched numbly as the Hawks halfback celebrated the try with high fives from his teammates. The freckly blond halfback turned in his direction and pumped his fist as the ref blew the whistle to signal full-time.

Just like that, the Ravens' brief winning streak was over.

< 69 >

# 11
# DOWN AND OUT

Junior sat in the Ravens change sheds by himself, slowly sipping from his water bottle and staring at the brick wall in front of him. Plastered on it were a dozen or so stickers shouting 'GO RAVENS!' in big black and green letters. He took a final sip, then placed his water bottle back in his bag. The other boys had already left, but Junior couldn't force himself off the bench. Two words kept echoing in his mind: *Fat chance*. It was

< 70 >

the Hawks halfback's parting shot to Junior.

The Ravens had been standing together after the game when the halfback and one of the Hawks forwards walked past, gloating. 'Guess we'll see you lot in the finals,' said the forward.

'*Fat* chance!' The halfback grinned. 'Get it?' The pair walked away, howling with laughter.

'I'm going to sort out that guy, once and for all!' said Tai. 'No one says that to our Cannonball and gets away with it!'

'No, you're not!' said Coach Steve, stopping Tai in his tracks. 'Look, there's always going to be a few jokers that sledge us. The important thing is that we don't

< 71 >

sink to their level. Remember, boys, it's not whether you win or lose –'

'We know – it's how you play the game,' groaned Corey, rolling his eyes.

'No, it's what you do *after* the game that matters,' corrected Coach. He looked around at each boy. 'Win or lose, you shake hands and show respect for your opponents. Even when – *especially when* – they don't respect you. Got it?'

'Yes, Coach,' the boys mumbled.

'Good. Now, get cleaned up,' said Coach Steve.

But while the rest of the boys had done just that, Junior had found it a little harder to simply shrug off the halfback's words. They were about him, after all.

< 72 >

Coach Steve poked his head into the change sheds. 'Junior, what are you still doing here? Your sister's waiting for you.'

Junior shrugged.

'Come on, mate, go home and get some rest,' said Coach Steve. 'Things always look a little brighter the day after a loss.'

'Okay, Coach,' Junior said quietly. But as he got to his feet and headed out the door, a new thought bounced around his brain.

*Maybe I don't want to be Cannonball anymore.*

< 73 >

# 12
# BILLY AT THE BEACH

Coach Steve had been right — things did look brighter the next day.

It was a clear, sunny morning when Junior and his family headed to the beach for a Taafuli family picnic. It was a weekly event that happened every Sunday. Most of the people at the picnic were related to Junior in some way or another. There were aunties, uncles, first, second *and* third cousins. But you didn't have to be part of the family to attend. You just had to enjoy eating.

< 74 >

Junior looked at the picnic tables, where his mother and aunties were busy preparing a traditional Samoan meal. Junior's dad and Uncle Lasalo had got up early to prepare the *umu*, which was basically a big hole in the ground filled with hot coals. It was how Samoans traditionally cooked their food. And the great thing was, you could cook a lot of food at the same time. Chicken, pork, fish, taro and breadfruit — enough for a feast!

Junior was busy breathing in the wonderful smoky smells of the *umu*-cooked food when a football hit him in the stomach. He looked up and saw his sister Ramona and his older cousin Fetu laughing wildly.

'Stop thinking about your stomach, cuz!'

< 75 >

said Fetu. 'Time for a game of footy before lunch, hey?'

Junior thought that yesterday's game might have turned him off playing with his uncles and cousins, but he couldn't say no. It was just too much fun. Because it was touch footy, Junior had to work hard to keep up with the speed of the game. Every second there were breaks and dummies and flick passes – anything that might draw a tackler in and create an overlap. It was all about ball skills, acceleration and timing. Junior always marvelled at the skills of his older cousins – both boys *and* girls. Even Mele and Ramona joined in, and they loved running rings around Junior and their two younger brothers.

< 76 >

'Did you hear about our Junior?' Ramona said to their uncle when they all took a break. 'Some kids on the other team are hassling him because they think he's too big!'

Junior glared at Ramona, embarrassed that she would bring it up in front of the whole family.

'What? This little fish?' replied their uncle, chuckling. 'If he jumped on my line, I'd throw him back!'

The funny thing was that Uncle Lasalo was quite a large man himself. He was at least twice the size of Junior. While Junior's father was tall and lean, like Joseph and Feleti, all the men on his mother's side were big and stout.

'Don't worry,' their cousin Fetu said to

< 77 >

Junior. 'They said the same thing to me when I played junior footy. Then I got even bigger and now nobody says anything.'

'It's not your fault you're big-boned and good at football,' said Uncle Lasalo. He slapped his stomach proudly. 'You take after your mother's brother. I was a great footballer, too!'

Everyone laughed at this, even Junior.

'Hey, isn't that Billy Slater?' said Mele. 'Your team's mascot.'

'He's their mentor, not their mascot,' corrected Ramona, shaking her head. She paused, squinting. 'Hey, I think it *is* him.'

Junior looked towards the beach. Approaching them, with a big group of men in training gear, was Billy Slater. Junior

< 78 >

wondered what Billy and his team were doing at the beach on a Sunday.

'Hey, Billy!' Mele shouted at the top of her lungs. Billy and the rest of the team turned to see her jumping up and down, pointing excitedly at Junior. 'My brother's in your team!' she screamed.

*What did she do that for?* thought Junior's brain, as the rest of him wilted with embarrassment.

But to his surprise, Billy waved back and began walking towards them.

*He's coming over. Billy's going to meet my family*, Junior thought with excitement. Then a second thought hit him like an air-to-surface missile.

*Oh, no, Billy's going to meet my mum!*

< 79 >

# SAMOAN PRIDE

'Hi Junior,' said Billy, glancing around at the Taafulis' picnic. 'Here with the family?'

'Yeah,' said Mele, before Junior could get a word out. 'You're Billy Slater, hey? Junior's mascot.'

'Mentor,' corrected Ramona, elbowing her sister in the side.

'Yeah, that too. I'm his *older* sister,' gushed Mele.

Junior rolled his eyes.

Billy smiled. 'It's nice to meet you . . .?'

< 80 >

'Mele.'

Ramona elbowed her again.

'Oh, yeah, this is Ramona, our other sister. And this is our family,' said Mele, waving her hand like a TV game show model. She then introduced Billy to every member of the Taafuli family. But if Billy was worried about being mobbed by a large group of over-friendly Samoans, he didn't show it.

'What are you doing down the beach, Billy?' asked Uncle Lasalo. 'You're a bit far from home.'

'We had a game last night and our coach thought a morning recovery session in the surf would be a good idea,' explained Billy.

'How's the water?' asked Fetu. 'Bit cold?'

'Freezing,' Billy agreed with a chuckle.

< 81 >

*Well, that could have gone worse*, concluded Junior. Billy was chatting and laughing with his family and he didn't look bored or annoyed or anything. *If I were a big footy star I'd hate people fussing over me.*

'Wow, cuz, you never told me you knew Billy Slater – the guy's a legend!' whispered Fetu.

In the back of his brain, Junior knew there was something he was forgetting, something big and important. Then suddenly it came to him. Or, rather, *she* came to him.

'So this is the famous foot-a-ball star Mr Billy Slater. The one who wants to tell me how to feed my son,' said Mama Taafuli. She seemed to appear from nowhere – another perfectly timed entrance.

< 82 >

'Oh, hi. You must be Mrs Taafuli,' Billy said awkwardly.

'Mama, you're embarrassing Junior,' Mele whispered loudly. Junior put his head in his hands. He couldn't bear to watch.

'That's all right, Mele,' said Billy. 'I guess you mean the Healthy Snack Challenge that I set the boys?' He'd faced a lot of tough oppositions in his football career and he could see that Mrs Taafuli was no pushover. She looked tough. Very tough. Her death-ray stare was set to kill.

'So, you think my son is unhealthy, hey? Something wrong with the food I give him?' said Mama Taafuli.

Junior peeked out from behind his hand and his worst fears were confirmed. His

< 83 >

mum was wagging her finger right in Billy Slater's face.

Billy just smiled politely. 'Well, that was just a challenge we set *all* the boys to encourage them to avoid junk food for a week. It wasn't really –'

But Mama Taafuli interrupted before Billy could finish. 'All right, I think *you* need to stay and try some proper Island food, and then you'll see how well Junior eats,' she said.

'Oh, that's very kind but –'

'No buts. Stay. Eat. You look too skinny to me, anyway.' Mama Taafuli laughed. 'How do you play football with such a little body?'

Billy couldn't help but smile. Junior's mum certainly spoke her mind and she didn't take no for an answer. Before he

< 84 >

knew it, she was handing him a plate and making him sample every single Samoan dish on the very crowded picnic table.

'This is amazing, Mrs Taafuli. What is it?' asked Billy, after sampling his first dish.

'Ahh, you mean my *palusami*. It's just taro leaves in coconut cream,' Junior's mum said with a satisfied smile.

'It's fantastic. And this pork is incredible, too,' said Billy. 'It's cooked in an emu, right?'

Everyone around the table burst into laughter. Junior's dad laughed so much he had tears in his eyes.

'We call it an *umu*,' corrected Mama Taafuli.

Billy gave an embarrassed smile. 'Right, good to know.'

< 85 >

'Wait till you try mum's *poi* — banana pudding,' said Junior. 'It's my favourite.'

'Can't wait,' said Billy. 'I do love my bananas.'

When lunch was over, Fetu brought out the footy again and Billy decided to stick around for a quick game of touch. Junior couldn't believe he was playing with a first-grade player. But after a few minutes, Billy became just another pair of hands — very quick hands.

Billy and Junior played on the same team, and like before, the game was fast and furious. And fun. At one point Billy completed a nice run around, passing it to Junior, who flicked the ball behind his back for Billy to sprint away over the make-shift tryline between two large pine trees.

< 86 >

But Billy didn't put the ball down to score. Instead, he waited for Junior to run through and do the honours.

'Nice ball work, Junior. You should try some of that in the next match,' Billy said after the game. 'You're not just a ball runner – you have some serious skills!' he added with a sincere nod.

'Yeah, maybe that will shut the other teams up!' said Fetu.

'What do you mean?' asked Billy.

'Some kids have been hassling Junior about his size,' said Ramona, 'just because they can't tackle him without using the whole team.'

'Is that true, Junior?' Billy asked with concern.

Junior nodded, the grin from scoring a try with Billy quickly fading from his face.

< 88 >

'Well, those kids don't know what they're talking about. Forwards are supposed to be hard to tackle, right?' said Billy.

'Yeah, I guess,' said Junior.

Billy patted him on the back. 'Trust me, I've faced some unfriendly opponents in my time. When you get out on that field, just do what comes naturally and be proud of who you are.'

'That's right. Samoan pride, cuz!' said Fetu.

Junior nodded. 'Thanks, Billy.'

As he waved goodbye after the game of touch, Junior hoped Billy was right. But a worm of doubt still lingered in his mind. *How can I be proud of myself?* thought Junior. *I'm not even sure who I am.*

< **89** >

# 14
# AND THE
# WINNER IS...

The night air was cool and the grass on the Ravens home ground was wet with dew as Junior and the rest of the team gathered around Coach Steve after another gruelling training session.

'Okay, lads, I know you've been hanging all session to find out about the Healthy Snack Challenge –'

'No, we haven't,' said Tai.

'I didn't ask you, did I?' said Coach. 'Now, make like a jacket and zip it.'

< 90 >

'Huh?' Tai said with a bewildered look.

Coach made a 'zipping' motion across his mouth and pointed at Tai, who finally got the point. 'Where was I?' said Coach.

'Healthy Snack Challenge,' said Tai.

'What did I just say?' Coach Steve shook his head in disbelief, making a few of the boys giggle. 'Anyway, the Healthy Snack Challenge . . . I'm going to let Billy tell you about it.'

'Thanks, Steve.' Billy stepped forward. 'Well, guys, the results were very interesting,' said Billy, a mysterious grin spreading across his face.

Junior sat at the back of the group. He hadn't said anything about bumping

< **91** >

into him at the beach, but Billy had given him a friendly wink at one point.

'Okay,' said Billy. 'You all did really well in making better choices when it came to snacks. Most of you were able to ditch the junk food for healthier options. The trick is to do that every week.'

'You want us to do that *every* week?' moaned Jackson.

'I want you to *try*. Listen, fellas, there's nothing wrong with having an occasional treat now and then, but it's much better for you to avoid consuming too much sugar and salt every day,' explained Billy. 'For example, instead of eating packets of chips, Ahmed ate cucumber sticks and hommus.'

'I'm Lebanese. We always eat cucumbers.'

< 92 >

Azza shrugged. 'Why do you think they call it the Lebanese cucumber?'

The boys laughed.

'Is anyone else getting hungry?' said Tai, earning another 'zip it' signal from Coach.

'And Junior,' continued Billy. 'He ate fruit every day and not one processed snack!'

'His dad works at the fruit markets,' announced Tai.

Junior didn't say anything, but a little wave of pride rippled over him.

'What's so good about fruit and vegetables, anyway?' said Corey. 'They grow in dirt.'

A few of the boys giggled.

'Well, that's how we know they're natural,' said Billy. 'You could use a few

< 93 >

more natural foods in your diet, Corey. The closest you came to eating a vegetable was chips.'

'Now I *really* am getting hungry,' said Tai. A little string of drool lined his lips.

'Coach Steve and I are so impressed with the effort you have all made, we're going to use your snack cards as raffle tickets to win this!' Billy held up a bulging shopping bag.

The boys all eyed the bag with excitement.

'What is it?' asked Blake.

Billy grinned. 'Let's find out.'

Coach Steve took off his Ravens cap and placed all the cards inside. He then gave the cards a swirl with his hand. Billy stuck his hand into the hat and pulled out a single yellow card. The whole team watched

< 94 >

anxiously as he unfolded the card and looked at the name.

'And the winner is . . . Junior Taafuli,' Billy announced proudly.

'No way,' said Corey.

'Yes way,' said Billy. 'Get up here and collect your prize, Junior.'

The youngest and biggest member of the team stood up, his face frozen in surprise. He made his way up to Billy with a giant smile on his face while the team waited anxiously to see what was in the bag.

< 95 >

# 15
# RAP ATTACK

'Here you go, mate,' said Billy, passing the shopping bag to Junior.

'Hurry up and open it!' yelled C. C.

'Yeah, we want to see what it is!' squealed Blake.

Junior opened the bag and pulled out a football. But the whole team could see it wasn't just an ordinary football.

'It's signed by the whole Australian squad,' said Billy.

Junior looked down at the ball in

< 96 >

his hands and the black squiggles of ink covering it. There were so many famous names he didn't know where to start.

'Enjoy,' said Billy. 'And keep eating healthy.'

The whole team clapped, and Junior couldn't help smiling. He couldn't wait to get home and show his family.

'All right, boys, that's all for today,' said Coach. 'Don't forget, nine o'clock Saturday morning at Craxton Oval.'

'Give us a look,' said Corey, as the boys moved off to the car park.

Junior hesitated. He didn't trust the Ravens centre, but he didn't want to seem spoiled either. He reluctantly handed the ball to Corey.

'Pretty cool,' said Corey. 'I can't believe

< **97** >

you won this in a dumb raffle. They should give it to the best player in the team, not the biggest.'

Junior could suddenly feel the anger building up in him like hot lava rising to the surface. He was Mount Taafuli and he was ready to explode. 'What's that supposed to mean?' he asked.

'Look, no offence, but you only play well because you're bigger than everyone else. It's not like you've got any real skill.'

'You're . . .' The lava was in Junior's throat now, but he couldn't get the words out.

'What?' said Corey. 'I'm just being honest.'

Junior stared at Corey, and Corey stared right back.

< 98 >

Finally, Junior broke the silence. 'You're wrong. Take it back,' he said through gritted teeth.

'Why? What are you going to do, Junior?' teased Corey.

Junior's face tightened and his hands balled into fists. He didn't want to do this but what choice did he have? He had to stand up for himself. He moved in closer to Corey. Corey stood there defiantly, tossing Junior's new football in his hands.

'Just you and me, big boy. Make your move,' said Corey.

Blake, who was standing on the hill waiting for his ride, noticed the stand-off and jumped into action. 'Fight! Fight! Junior and Corey are going to *fight*!'

< **99** >

That was enough to send the rest of the boys racing back down to the field.

Corey and Junior were standing in a sea of white from the floodlight overhead. Suddenly, they were surrounded by half-a-dozen boys.

'What are you waiting for?' taunted Corey.

Junior closed his eyes and took a deep breath.

'Thought so. You're just a big marshmallow – SOFT.'

Junior cut loose. 'I'm fat.'

'What?' Corey's forehead creased in confusion.

*I said I'm fat,*
*like a Cheshire cat*

< 100 >

*with riddles and rhymes. Can you deal with
    that?*

*I'm BIG*

*as a rocket ship.*

*I'm blasting to the moon. You're going nowhere
    quick.*

*I'm E-NOR-MUS. I'm a super-sized sun.*

*You're a tiny little planet OR-BIT-ING my
    bum.*

*Yeah, you're skinny on manners and you're
    light on respect.*

*I got news for you, boy, you're gonna hit the
    deck*

*when you turn around*

*and watch me claim the crown,*

*like Humpty on that wall, you know you're
    gonna fall down.*

< 101 >

*'Cause I'm Poly-born and I'm Poly-proud,*
*and I'm not afraid to shout it out loud.*
*I'm a Samoan-at-LARGE and I'm here to stay.*
*So shut your mouth, there's nothin' left to say.*
*Word!'*

Corey was gobsmacked. The rest of the boys burst into applause, whistling and cheering. Junior had no idea where it had come from, and he didn't care. It felt amazing. He would never have been able to say that to Corey or anyone else before, but he could rap it.

'That was . . .' began Corey.

'AWESOME!' said Tai.

'Weird,' Corey said finally. 'I'm going home . . . to get away from you losers,' he said softly and slinked off into the darkness.

< **103** >

'I guess we'll just add that to your growing list of talents, Junior,' said Coach Steve.

Junior turned around to see Coach and Billy standing behind him.

'For a second there I thought I was going to have to break up a fight, but I wasn't about to get caught up in a rap battle,' Coach said with a laugh.

Junior's face went bright red. 'Sorry, Coach, he just got to me . . .'

'I know, he has that effect sometimes. He needs to work on his people skills. But it was good to see you solving it with words instead of fists. Or was it just WORD?' joked Coach.

Billy shook his head at Coach's attempted humour and winked at Junior. 'Nice one,

< **104** >

mate. I'm more into rock music, but you may have converted me.'

As the rest of the team headed to the car park, Junior took a final look around the Ravens home ground. He wondered if he'd be able to stand up for himself on Saturday if the opposition teased him, or whether he should just ignore them. He thought about Billy's words from the picnic: *Do what comes naturally.* Was it really that simple?

One way or another he'd find out on Saturday, when the Ravens took on the Comets.

< 105 >

# 16
# WHERE ARE THE ORANGES?

As it happened, doing what came naturally wasn't that simple.

Most of Junior's family had turned up at the game to watch him, and even Billy Slater was there. But for some reason, Junior was having one of the worst games ever. Whenever he got the ball, he couldn't decide what to do. *Smash through the defence? Off-load? Why can't I just play naturally?*

It didn't help when some of the Comets

< **106** >

forwards decided to offer their own opinions on his form.

'I thought number ten was supposed to be unstoppable?' said a large second rower.

'Yeah?' replied another Comet. 'News-flash — we just stopped him!'

These guys weren't teasing him about his size, they were making fun of his skills!

'Come on, Junior, fire up!' Uncle Lasalo called from the sideline.

But Junior felt like he had nothing left to ignite him. The rest of the Ravens weren't playing well, either. Their attack was flat and their defence less than impressive. No one seemed to be able to get into second gear. When the half-time whistle blew, the Comets led 20–0.

< 107 >

To top it off, Tai had rolled his ankle trying to evade a tackle on the last play of the first half. He'd limped off the field and was now sitting in front of Coach Steve with his football boot off and his ankle swollen like a party balloon.

'Well, that did *not* go to plan,' said Coach Steve. 'And I don't think I can send you back out there on that ankle, Tai,' he added. 'Get ready, Ravi. You're up.'

Ravi, who was still struggling to tape up his socks without taping his hands to his boots, gulped.

Coach sighed. 'I thought we had a good chance today. The Comets haven't won a game all season, we should be blitzing them.'

< 108 >

'Coach?' Liam said gently. 'Sorry to interrupt, but where are the oranges?'

'Where's the what? Oh.' Coach looked around at the boys, then back at Liam. 'I . . . think I forgot the oranges.'

The boys groaned.

'Sorry, guys,' said Coach, hanging his head. He'd never, in his five years of coaching, forgotten the half-time oranges.

'We're down 20–0, I'm out of the game *and* we don't have oranges. What else can go wrong?' said Tai.

Junior had to agree. But maybe there were worse things than not playing footy — like playing really badly. And in front of your family, too.

Suddenly, Junior had a brilliant idea.

< **109** >

'Brilliant idea, Junior!' said Billy.

Junior looked around at his teammates munching on bananas, and smiled. He had remembered seeing a few boxes of them in the family van. While they weren't oranges, the team seemed grateful for the much-needed energy boost.

'So, what do you reckon is going wrong out there?' asked Billy.

'Don't know,' said Junior. But that wasn't quite true. 'I guess I don't want to be the human cannonball anymore. I don't want to be the big kid no one can tackle.'

'Junior, you're much more than that,' said Billy. 'One thing I know about footy

< 110 >

is there's always another way.'

Junior shrugged.

'All right, boys, up and at 'em!' said Coach, managing to rustle up some new-found enthusiasm. 'What about those bananas, hey? Lucky Junior's dad was here.'

'It sure is different,' said Tai, flinging his banana peel at Blake. 'I suppose it's good to mix it up a bit.'

'Mix it up?' said Billy. 'Tai, you're a genius!'

'Thank you,' replied Tai, right before his own banana skin landed back on his head.

Billy smiled. 'Junior, I think I just had a brilliant idea of my own.'

< 111 >

# 17
# BANANA KICK

'I hope this works,' said Coach Steve.

'Me too,' Billy said nervously, as he watched the Ravens get into position for the start of the second half.

The Comets kicked off and the ball sailed straight to C. C., who took it on the full and ran it up to the twenty-metre line before being tackled. Jackson took the next hit up and made a few metres. Then Poppa ran the ball up on the third tackle and made a little more ground before being brought

< 112 >

down. Next, Liam made a squirreling run through the middle and off-loaded to Junior, who was standing further down the line of attack than usual.

When the defence saw Junior with the ball, they pounced. But by the time the Comets got to Junior, he no longer had the ball. He'd passed back to Blake, who accelerated through the gap left by the defenders. Blake drew another two in, then passed to Nick Raco, who took off down the sideline in a blur and didn't stop until he was diving over to score.

The Ravens fans broke into wild cheers.

'Way to go, Junior!' called Mele and Ramona from the sideline.

< 113 >

'Well, what do you know,' said Coach Steve.

'Long way to go yet,' said Billy, a wide grin now on his face.

All the team had needed was a little change. Billy had asked Coach Steve to put Ravi into the forwards and Junior to five-eighth. Everyone in the team, including Coach Steve, had been puzzled by Billy's suggestion. Everyone except for Junior. He'd known exactly what Billy was thinking. And when the Ravens crossed for their second try ten minutes later, Junior knew Billy's idea was working.

This time, Junior had made a strong bust from halfway and found Liam coming

< 115 >

back on the inside. Junior took on three Comets players before he flick-passed the ball back to Liam. It caught the Comets by surprise. Liam took advantage of this, passing the ball to C. C., who burst through a tackle and found Josh faithfully backing up.

Josh scored his second try of the season, and suddenly the Ravens were back in it. Junior could finally feel himself relax. He wasn't worried about what everyone was saying. It was as if the rules had changed. As five-eighth, Junior had to keep the ball on the move. It was just like playing touch footy with his uncles and cousins — as long as he had quick hands and timing,

< 116 >

he could leave the acceleration to his speedy teammates.

But it wasn't just Junior's ball skills that had lifted the team. The Ravens could smell a win. The team hadn't just found second gear, they'd hit the turbo button. With ten minutes to go, Jack teamed up with Azza for their own run five metres out from the tryline.

Azza passed the ball back to Jack, who palmed off two defenders and held up a pass for Poppa. Poppa smashed his way through the line defence and scored straight under the posts. The easy conversion brought the score to 16–18.

< 117 >

The Ravens were close, but they were running out of time. The clock was ticking down, and the Comets weren't about to roll over that easily. They did their best to keep the Ravens in their own half for the next five minutes. Even Junior couldn't bust through the line or get the ball away. The Comets had wised up to his off-loads and were now smothering the ball in their three-man tackles.

< 118 >

With a few minutes to go, the Ravens were feeling desperate. They'd come so close, but it looked like they were going to fall short.

'We need some magic, boys!' said Liam, his eyes locking on Junior.

Junior nodded. If he couldn't break the line with his body or his off-loads, what else was there? He looked to the crowd for assistance. All he saw were the anxious faces of his family. His uncle and aunt, his cousin Fetu, his brothers and sisters – even his mum was gripping his dad's arm for dear life. 'Come on, Junior!' she cheered. 'You can do it!'

Then he saw the empty fruit box by his dad's feet. That's it! 'Banana,' he mumbled.

< **119** >

'What?' Corey said sharply.

'Banana!' repeated Junior.

'Yeah, I get it. Your dad gave us bananas,' said Corey, with more than a hint of sarcasm.

'No . . .' Junior looked at Corey. There was no glare or death-ray stare, just the look of one teammate to another. A look that said *Trust me.* 'Banana,' he repeated slowly, pointing to the sky.

'*Oh*,' said Corey, as Junior's plan finally dawned on him. 'Yeah, do it!'

Junior moved into position behind the pack and Corey headed out wide. 'I want the last,' Junior whispered to Liam.

Liam nodded. 'All right.'

The referee signalled the fifth and last and Azza passed the ball from dummy half

< 120 >

straight to Liam. The Comets prepared for the kick. Liam always kicked on the last.

But not this time.

He sucked in some defenders and tossed the ball behind him to Junior.

'What's he doing?' cried Coach Steve.

Billy shrugged his shoulders.

Junior glanced over at Corey, who was lining up with him on the far right side of the field. He had done this plenty of times with his brothers in the backyard, and even a few times playing touch with his cousins, but never in a real game.

*Please work*, he prayed as two Craxton forwards moved in to tackle him. Junior reversed his grip on the ball, then kicked it. The ball spiralled away. The Comets

< 121 >

forwards barrelled into Junior, taking him to the ground. Junior hardly noticed. He was too busy watching the ball.

Instead of going straight over the heads of the Comets players like everyone was expecting, it curved to the right and into

the hands of Corey, who had leapt through the air and caught the ball with the tips of his fingers.

A perfect banana kick.

# 18
# A BIG FUTURE

'Sorry, boys,' said Junior, showing his empty hands to the two Comets players who had tackled him.

They both turned to see Corey with the ball, racing away down the sideline. Junior had pulled off a magic trick, after all. Corey scored in the corner, and the Ravens fans erupted. The team rushed over and jumped on Corey. Then they turned around and charged at Junior.

'Pick him up!' someone cried, and

< 124 >

the team tried to get Junior up on their shoulders.

'Not going to happen,' said Junior. But they did manage to get his feet a little off the ground before he collapsed on top of them.

'Hey, get off me!' Blake yelled from the bottom of the pile of tangled bodies, and the rest of the team laughed.

Liam's goal conversion was unsuccessful, but when the whistle blew it didn't matter. The Ravens had won.

'Well done, Junior,' said Coach Steve. 'You really worked some magic out there today.'

'That's why we call him Mr Magic,' said Tai.

< 125 >

'I thought it was Cannonball?' said Coach. Tai shook his head. 'Coach, keep up.'

'But . . .' began Coach. Then Tai and Junior cracked up, and he realised he'd been had. 'Hey, what's going on over there?' Coach pointed at Mama Taafuli. She was busy handing a stack of plastic containers to Billy.

'. . . and this is my *palusami* that you liked and this one has the *poi*, Junior's favourite. And here's some more *umu*-cooked pork. Just a thank-you for everything you've done for Junior,' said Mama Taafuli.

'Um, thank you,' said a surprised but grateful Billy.

'Hey, Mrs Taafuli, when can I sample some of your cooking?' called Coach Steve.

< **126** >

'This one here is still skinny,' said Mama Taafuli, pointing at Billy. 'Looks to me like you sampled too many dishes already.'

The surrounding crowd of players and family laughed at this, and Coach Steve shook his head.

'What is this, Pick-on-Coach-Steve Day?' he said.

'Just jokes, Coach,' said Tai. 'Don't be so serious.'

Junior laughed and looked around at his family and his team. Finally, things felt right. He didn't have to be The Big Kid or even Cannonball. He was Junior Taafuli. He could rap and he could play footy, and no matter what anyone said, Junior knew he had a big future ahead of him.

< **127** >

'Hey, is anyone else hungry?' asked Tai. 'Maybe we should order a pizza.'

Coach Steve sighed. 'Unbelievable.'

It was going to be a very long season.

< 128 >

1. Fullback: Cameron 'C.C.' Cotter

2. Winger: Nick Raco

3. Centre: Blake 'The Fake' Vargas

4. Centre: Corey Wilson

5. Winger: Josh Brown

6. Five-Eighth: Tai Nguyen

7. Halfback: Liam McGill

8. Prop Forward: Junior 'Cannonball' Taafuli

9. Hooker: Ahmed 'Azza' Azzi

10. Prop Forward: Lucas 'Poppa' Popovic

11. Second Row: Matthew 'Michael' Miller

12. Second Row: Jackson Miller

13. Lock Forward: Jack Monroe

Reserve: Ravi Rangarajan

Coach: Steve Smith

**Junior**
**TAAFULI**

AGE: 10

WEIGHT: 59 kg

HEIGHT: 160 cm

POSITION: Prop forward

Junior is the youngest player on the team, and he is also the biggest. His tackle-busting line breaks have earned him the nickname Cannonball. But don't be fooled by his size. This forward has some pretty handy ball skills and a tricky little flick pass, too. Junior can win a game almost single-handedly, but prefers to throw the ball around with his teammates and rely on his skill, rather than his size. When he's not breaking tackles, this unlikely rapper is busting rhymes. Word!

AGE: 10
HEIGHT: 145 cm
WEIGHT: 42 kg
POSITION: Winger

An inexperienced but speedy player, what Josh lacks in confidence and size, he makes up for in heart. Josh is a great support player and, given a chance, he will tear away down the sideline. Expect lots of points from this galloping winger before the season is over – once he gets his ball-handling under control.

Josh's interests include football and his fave food is a classic barbecued sausage sandwich – don't forget the tomato sauce.

AGE: 11
HEIGHT: 152 cm
WEIGHT: 45 kg
POSITION: Centre

Corey's motormouth may get him into a bit of trouble with his teammates, but this fiery centre is the team's speed demon. Corey is a deadset try machine with a killer sidestep, although he does have a tendency to go 'one out' a little too often.

Besides playing footy, Corey helps his mum make ends meet by delivering Crazee Bargains catalogues. He's pretty handy on a skateboard as well.

Ravi is super-smart and can rattle off any footy statistic or piece of trivia about the game you can throw at him. Just don't throw him the football — his skills are a little on the under-developed side. But with a little confidence and coaching, Ravi's natural intelligence and enthusiasm for footy may convert to points on the board before the season ends.

Ravi is a self-confessed maths geek and prides himself on knowing more footy facts than a TV commentary team.

AGE: 10
HEIGHT: 147 cm
WEIGHT: 41 kg
POSITION: Reserve

He might be the team's smallest player but this pocket rocket half is the Ravens' engine. Without Liam calling the plays and driving his teammates forward, the Ravens would get nowhere. His lightning reflexes and natural instinct for the game make Liam the Ravens' MVP — most valuable player.

Liam's interests include footy, footy and more footy.

AGE: 11
HEIGHT: 140 cm
WEIGHT: 38 kg
POSITION: Halfback and
Team Captain

## Healthy Eating

Eating the right food will not only benefit your health, it can also help to improve your fitness and skill level. For sports stars, and those starting out in sport, a nutritious, well-balanced diet can boost your performance and aid with recovery.

### *Key points*

 Try to maintain a balanced diet of fruit and vegetables, protein (such as lean meats, fish and eggs) and carbohydrates (such as

wholegrain cereals, oats, wholegrain bread and pasta). This will ensure your body receives the right vitamins and minerals for growth and development.

- Drink plenty of water when exercising to stay hydrated.

- Avoid overeating junk food, such as fried foods, chocolate, chips, cake and other sweets. While they provide energy, they are often high in sugar and low in nutrition.

- When you need an energy boost before or during exercise, try to stick to fruit. For example, bananas are high in potassium, Vitamin B6, Vitamin C and fibre. They are also a natural source of carbohydrate for when you need a long-lasting shot of energy to keep you firing. As an ambassador for bananas, I'm a big fan of snacking on them when I'm training or before a big game.

## The Banana Kick

The banana kick is a punt kick that curves away from the kicker rather than travelling in a straight line. It is a difficult kick to get right but a handy one to know because of its unpredictable 'banana' curve. This can fool your opposition and give you an edge when attempting to regather.

### *Key points*

- Line up your kick as you normally would to kick straight, holding the ball out as you prepare to kick. Turn the ball on a 45-degree angle so that when your foot strikes the ball it cuts across the *side* of the ball. Strike the ball hard using the outside of your boot. The ball should curve away from your leg.

You will need to practise this kick a lot to get it right. Try doing this over small distances in the backyard or the park. Have a friend stand in the direction you want to curve the ball. Be patient, and you should soon be kicking bananas all over the park!

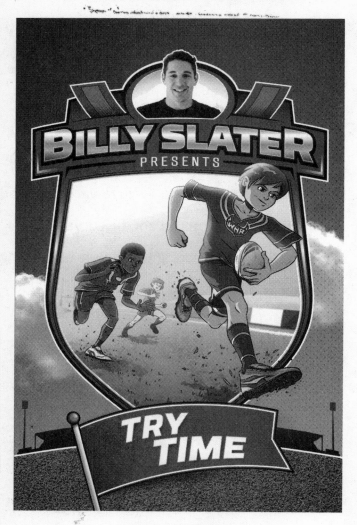

AVAILABLE NOW

MORE GREAT BILLY SLATER BOOKS COMING SOON!